MADONNA
WHO SHIFTS
FOR HERSELF

Lyn Lifshin

ACKNOWLEDGMENTS

Some of the poems previously in: *Wormwood Review,
Rolling Stone, Minotaur, Poetry Now, Peqyod, Sing
Heavenly Muse, Granite* and *Maelstrom Review.*

Cover photo by Gretchen Rarsai

Library of Congress Cataloging in Publication Data

Lifshin, Lyn
    Madonna who shifts for herself.

    I. Title.
PS3562.I4537M3 1983   811'.54   82-73945
ISBN 0-930090-19-5 (lim. ed.)
ISBN 0-930090-18-7 (pbk.)

APPLEZABA PRESS
P.O. Box 4134
Long Beach, CA 90804

I.

SHIFTING FOR HERSELF MADONNA

wants her hand on

the stick to

tell it how

to go she

wants to eat

power come

down hard shifty

and thrifty

and fast

at pulling out

PEDESTAL MADONNA

    he puts her up
on a pedestal
and she goes
down on it

NON RETURNABLE BOTTLE MADONNA

when she's cold
and glistens all
men want her
hold her greedy
in their hands
their mouths
parched and ready

she goes
down good
tastes right,
pleases

but if the men
don't have to
pay they don't
care what
happens throw

her out leave
her abandoned
on some back
road, trash

CHANUKAH MADONNA

burns too fast

gets brighter
throughout
the week

her wick waiting
for the match
that will burn

her to nothing

STRIPPER MADONNA

sticks her tongue out
lying on the dusty mat
it looks long
as a boa

flicks her g-string
so the elastic
triangle wriggles

you can see the up
and down scar,
a bruise

spreads her cheeks in
the mirror   local
melons the round
musky kind   now she's

moving her hand up
and down as if a
cock was in it

in front of the satin

when she groans

you half believe

she wants

to be here

BACKWARDS STRIPPING MADONNA

she starts with her
cunt hairs flashing
a little split when she
asks can you smell
me in the back row.
this is ordinary.
now she pulls a satin
patch over her patch,
puts on her shoes.
now it gets wilder.
the music speeds up
like her clothes a
black full skirt
floats no it flies in
circles a strip of
gold to hide her ass.
now she's spinning so
fast a gipsy in
front of the fire
that comes out of
red light hitting the
old man's vodka, giving
her color she doesn't
have

ANOTHER BACKWARD STRIPPER MADONNA

this one looks better
with her clothes on
knows   slides from
a quilt into rolled
up panty hose quick
while he's in the
shower then she
grabs her jeans she's
under a hundred lbs
but she still feels
fat   only goes to
pee if all the lights
are off

STRIPPER MADONNA

has on a little
patch of satin   twists
to a scratchy tape
Dolly Parton's here
you come

a whirl of tulle
the place smells of
tabu and a little
Raid   she

spreads her legs
like a wish
bone cracking

offers to clean
your glasses
sucks them deep
inside those
frizzy lips

the next few days
smell like Friday

TIN CAN MADONNA

loud, flashy and trashy

JULY MADONNA

is hot

but when she's
threatened
pulls in deep you
know she won't
talk becomes
hard and crabby,
her own shell

MADONNA NYMPHOMANIA

raw, red and ready

JEALOUS MADONNA

he mentions a
stacked blonde and
madonna can't sleep
dreams cornstalks
enormous as Kansas
pressing her 32 B
lovely littles in
to herself and
out the back like a
double hunchback

PUSHY PUSSY MADONNA

uses what
she can
rubs up against
especially when
she's hungry
but keeps her claws out
of sight   plays
with you a little
a game you
think as she
moves in for the
kill

GYM SEAL MADONNA

bubbly in the
night then
cool, glassy
and hard if no
thing touches
her by morning

SHEET ROCK MADONNA

is very stiff
until she gets
wet   then
she crumbles

MADONNA OF THE DEMOLITION DERBY

is fast   a
little jerky
she rams her ass
up against
and doesn't look
where she's
going   loud
getting knocked
up and down
you can see
where she's been

MINESTRONE MADONNA

cuts you in
to little pieces
and lets you boil
in your own juice

BLOOD RED NAIL POLISH MADONNA

she covers up
is hard glassy
and bold, a
little chippy

JELLY MADONNA

a good bed
spread that
covers you

SOIL PIPE MADONNA

she eats shit

STAMP MADONNA

licks and smoothes
your sticky edges
and sends you

PUSSY MADONNA

singing the pussy
blues   but pussy
as in pus   not
pussy   something
inside that has
to get out and
can't   being
mostly thought
of as pussy

PARACHUTE MADONNA

either quite manic
or depressive
either up and flying
or down with a
huge crash

RADIATOR MADONNA

you can sit
on her but take
it slow

she reminds you of
old places   you

lean your ass
into her   she's

hot stuff   good
and loud she
wants you to
make her bleed

but she could burn you

MOLD MADONNA

she's been down
so long in
her damp dark
she smells of
rooms bandaged
from the light
comes apart if
you touch her

MONONGAHELA MADONNA

flows and goes

DOVE TAILED MADONNA

is old but
is made better

expensive
but smooth

once you're in
her feathers
you're in to stay

MADONNA ANOREXIA NERVOSA

weighs 68 pounds
lives on lettuce
feels fat when
she even sees
a peach she's
too thin to have
a baby wants to
stay a baby
slips thru your
fingers

SLUG MADONNA

moves slow
stays in the dark
moist places
of your heart

she seems soft,
like plastic pipe
that's easy
to bend

easy to gulp down
as a shot of rum
or bourbon

she is her
own shell,
metal inside
a bullet

MADONNA'S FINGER ON HIM

makes it
glow   makes
it grow

THE HEPPLEWHITE MADONNA

rare, hard to
find   expensive yes
but lasts

gets better
with age

MADONNA WHO WRITES TEN POEMS A DAY

as if the poems were
vitamins she spits
out instead of
swallowing   one poem
gets the blue out
of her   calms like
vitamin B   another
heals   makes for
good sex supposedly
Others make bones
and muscles
stronger   cure
night blindness
protect   grow hair

GOODBY MADONNA

it was like opening
your mouth for steak
when you're starved
and finding it glued
tight to a huge
gushing sewer

the kiss was of a
porcupine in flight
a skunk dying   When

he said i really like
you he had the letters
changed around one
"l" missing "kill"
not "kiss" or "like"

II.

IF YOU GO POKING AROUND IN MY JOURNAL
YOU DESERVE THE WORST

like a rapist
who gets v.d.

poke and push your
self into any
thing of mine
when I'm not
aware or
willing

you deserve the
ugliest you
are raping
what I might
have opened to you

WITH YOU

i could feel ice
crystals on my thigh
cold barnacles

sometimes the ice got
thick and i couldn't
see   i dreamed of
bruise blue flowers

i was an herb cubed in
an ice you could
dissolve and use as
it was convenient

fish in lake the water
freezes over i
was your violet jelly
under paraffin

waiting to be
opened, spread, gulped down

42

ROOMATES

wondering what "it"
would be like in the
pea green stucco
rooms with plate
glass windows
wondering how far to
go Dorothy back
after losing 40
lbs and having her
nose fixed with
new boys who
wanted to touch
her there and there
and I didn't know what
to do about Joel
Schildkraut's
finger above the
waist was one thing
One week in the Phi
Sig house after one
beer I let his
hand slide down
there my period
stopped 11 weeks

wouldn't come like a
red flower down my
leg in the snow until
walking down Euclid
to East Gennesee with
a fake name Sherry
Russell I picked
a doctor out of
a book and with my
legs in the stirrups
blushed   said whiskey
and no I wouldn't name
the boy I guess
my hymen was like a
pink paraffin lid
no need to worry he
shook his head for
5 dollars in crumpled
hot sweaty ones

NUNS AT A RETREAT

they'd hoist up their black
skirts she said years
later when she left it
was like a group of children
or strange birds all
ruffling black feathers
letting their black stockinged
legs dry off as they kicked
on the stones
looking at each other's
thighs and calves it was
as if the sun was making
love to them

POET AS STRIPPER

they assume more,
no matter what you're like
off the stage
of the poem
they concentrate on your
darkest black places
they'll clap and holler
hoping to see something snap

call after midnight
see you living in some
sleazy walk up flat
that smells of patchouly
musk and skin
dark with the shades drawn

they write requesting
your used underwear
some stained nylon crotch
publishers want to
call your book "Undressed"
pose you nude in corn
stalks shave what
they think shouldn't show

some pretend to be bored
by what you reveal
"Overexposed" one critic
calls out wanting to
rewrite your end

they want to know your age
the shape you're in

it's your skin
they're after   sure they
can get inside
they dream your smell
on their fingers

you're just a super·
cock tease if you're
not what you write

THE MAN WHO BROUGHT THE EMERALD
MANDARINS

carried me up the
three flights the
first night   touched
my left nipple   I
never trust men so
charming   sea eyes
color of freezing and
gulped vodka in the
bathroom   wrapped
in that glass 2 nights
as "I'll never get
over those blue eyes"
stuck on the record
touched myself wanting
his smell   knowing
this will change
like the emerald mandarins
already looking like
ordinary oranges

ALONE ON A BLANKET

i feel shy un
sure of myself
as i was
at 15 i still
feel my legs
are too fat tho
my thighs are
19 inches and
people still
ask me for my
i.d. Blues
gnaw saturday
like sand on
wood tho i know
being over 30
shouldnt matter
look men right
in their eyes
tho the sun
glares so
then i paste
my books around
me write notes
on my skin so
no one can

see where i
am but i feel
my legs still
betray me
Without my own
man these men
with their
hard brown legs
look like some
exotic lobster
i'm served ½
started to eat
tho i dont know
how to crack
the shell if its
too messy or if
i want to

HAIR

beowulf's widow let
hers flow loose
when her husband
died like some mid
west plains indians
flowing wild like
grass like grief
the braid of the
dead man cut from
the corpse put in
a sacred bundle
with braids of his
other dead family
carried by his woman
when she'd
move like the hair
wreaths in new
england 50 years
of a gone family
braided together
under glass locked
and hung over the
fire as a painting

some photo grabbed
running in the
snow with the guns
the drums coming

HEAD OF THE STATE PARKS POLICE

with his 500 page
book on just how
to draw penises
his radio receiver
built in right next
to his bed   one in
the bathroom   he
listens in off duty
listens to the boys
won't take a vacation
maybe a few hours
off to take close up
shots of snatch in
Hustler   blow them
up for on the wall
next to the finger
that says stick this
up and turn it on
the dildo he uses
to hang his hat

SATURDAY

huge bed just
my outline in it.
the dreams pulled
into poems, dark
apples   a red
maple collapsing
with rain

things in me like
blind mice running
into each other

THE WOMAN WHO BURIES

her head in his lap
swallowing the cock
down letting his
nest blind her hot
sun she'll miss
the new willows
sweating feeling
the steering wheel
bump her shoulder
he's in control
she feels her belly
turn wishes he'd
hurry but won't
sit up till he's
come a woman like
this doesn't want to
see where she's going

NOT LETTING YOU SEE WHAT YOU DON'T
WANT TO

I gulped wine down fast
hearing your car
cut thru hard snow

maybe i'm the one
who wants to keep
things as separate as
rooms in a Japanese house

won't let you hear
crying thru thin
partitions half
of me is hidden

from you like some
one who lives on
his back the moons
of his ass pale,
invisible you

might think he didn't
still have them
in the Figi Island
under a blood hot sun

56

THE DREAM OF THE GUILT BIRD, OR WATER

there's too much water in the
tub or maybe something
is broken water
leaking out on the

mahogeny floor so the famous
playwrite comes in   trips
then they find out it
was me by one small

dark hair near the
drain i have to leave no
more studio in the
trees no more

peanut butter and lettuce
no more birds they
repossess the poems i
didn't write revise

july they are suing my
yellow maverick
a girl who isn't me
but is wearing my clothes

sits at my typewriter
she has given up baths and
shaved her hair
the guilt bird sits on

her shoulder swallows her
words she dreams she'll
always be writing
about this

HYSTERIA

nothing nice in this
huge centipede   you find
him with a million legs
of course it's a him
at least around midnight
snoring and waving legs
in your mouth   legs like
a hundred pricks and you're
a one hour past virgin
gangbanged by the Baltimore
Orioles, all of them seven
times their size   none
with just one penis

JEALOUSY

a fart that
smells up the room,
you pretend you're
not the one
but your cheeks are fire

you imagine it's a dark
green cloud
outlined like words in
a comic strip in a room
that's shrinking fast

ONE MORNING

even before it's light
tweezers will sprout thru your
new blue indian print sheets

you'll be lying there
the first saturday alone since
october when you painted
frost over the garage
so no one could tell if
you were home

the tweezers grow four inches
in seconds   even the maple
can't distract you now
you've left the garage open
dental floss whips around

your throat tighter than
your cousin's expert lips
a tooth bigger than all the
ones you've lost blocks
the door   a knot of

floss across your eyes
as the dresser handles
fling themselves sideways
across the room at the
angle of a penis
to cover you for good

JEALOUSY

you show a little and
then they clap
taunt   whistle more

it's a stripper
who's given a little
wink   who knows who

means what.
it seems like a
come on   some
thing sure

once you start you'll
be naked in your
flat beer

things exposed
you hadn't planned to

THE SECRET EATER

                    who doesn't share
and it's not mostly
pussy in fact
he's not very
secret about that,
leaves letters full
of teeth marks
on every desk
some tell of a
little v.d. sandwich

I stayed in his
house seven days and
never got offered coffee
he'd leave at 6 am
for a class
around eleven
came back smelling of
meatballs
stew.

I only found a vanilla
toffee. By the fifth day
I was dreaming of hamburg

ate 4 slices of rye
sprinkled with salt
to not pass out
I didn't mind him
running back to
his wife
just longed for
a doggy bag

One night I went out
for an interview
and packed my boots
with caviar   apricots
nuts   I should

have known the
first night   he ate
till he threw up
while I dumbly
nibbled a 45
cent salad

thinking of another huge poet
whose wife had said
I'd offer you
a donut but we only
have 12 left
for ourselves

one night he ordered
four servings
of french fries
stoned on my acid
then asked me
to pay the bill

I could hear him
swelling past his
clothes buttons clicked
like nails he ran out

came back hours later
crumbs a little
mustard on his head
I pretended to
be sleeping

seams split like a
house on fire
the zipper's teeth

I burrowed under
the covers pretending
to snore I

knew the only thing
he wanted me to eat
was him

66

THE WOMAN WHO COLLECTS BOXES

doesn't know what
to keep or what
to bury. She wraps
her house around
her, gets stoned on
auctions lugs back
a huge box she
could hide in. Boxes
stained with tar
One box has buttons
carved on it and
nails. A glass one
painted with an
animal with wings
One has a rusty
key None of them
haven't been used
One seems burned
from some war.
The boxes may be
the way she sees
her history
the box she thought
no one could ever

open, would want
to stay inside
She had trouble
changing no's to
know, still has
trouble saying
yes except in the
poems she keeps
in a box that's
like a crib or
is it a coffin
Is she hoarding
or separating
things she can't
fix or take back
like a lie that
becomes what is
in a poem some
lover eats

MEN AND PUBLISHERS

when i was looking for a
man or men and sat a
round waiting for the
phone   sat fat on the
bleachers in the gym
wanting to be a
honey   no one asked
me to dance

i didn't want to marry and
that limp cock pushed
whispered should

when he thought i wanted him
to stay you know
he kept running

i was waiting for the mail
waiting for the car
lights all that year the
bell that didn't

and i did it again
this fall waiting about
the book waiting for one
of the biggies to
eat you'd think it had
been my cunt

those awful slips with
him for dinner we like your
legs but we are full

in one week the divorce and
the publishing house i'd been
waiting for twelve months
wrote back sweety no

I decided the men could
wait for me I couldn't
keep waiting now they line
up some of them camp
near my study i

don't even have time now
to think of the book

know when i stop thinking
wondering well i know
contracts will come pushing
themselves on me like a
midnight cock when i just
wanted a little sleep

THE MIDWEST IS FULL OF VIBRATORS

you don't see them right off,
kind of the way grass ripples
in the prairie and you know
something's moving and then
it stops and starts again

love in the flat lands
matters more the sky is
so huge it swallows,
claustrophobic as a
giant diaphram

in the midwest they
think the east is smirking.
I could curl up for years
in a drawer where those
vibrators are kept

under flannel waiting
for a tongue to spin
me smooth take me out of
my razzle dazzle New York
clothes somebody who

wouldn't say much
or talk fast and nervously
as I do   someone slow
and hypnotic as an
Indiana tornado

OTHER BOOKS FROM APPLEZABA PRESS:

-THE BEACH AT CLEONE(poetry) Toby Lurie ($3.95)
-THE HANDYMAN POEMS(poetry) Leo Mailman ($3.95)
-THE RAW-ROBED FEW(poetry) Guy R. Beining
-HISTORICAL DOCUMENT(fiction) Nichola Manning($3.95)
-FRENCHWOMAN POEMS (poetry) Nichola Manning ($1.50)
-BOVVER ART(poetry) Nichola Manning ($2.50)
-THE CURE: a novel for speed readers(fiction) Gerald
                                        Locklin($2.75)
-SCENES FROM A SECOND ADOLESCENCE(poetry) Gerald
                                        Locklin ($3.95)
-DRIVING TO HERE(poetry) David James ($2.50)
-SURFACE STREETS(poetry) David James ($3.95)
-VIDEO POEMS(poetry) Billy Collins ($2.50)
-MOG & GLOG (fiction) d.h. lloyd (2.25)
-IF GRAVITY WASN'T DISCOVERED(poetry) d.h. lloyd ($1.50)
-STRIPTEASE and other poems(poetry) Elliot Fried ($2.00)
-BAD SMOKE GOOD BODY(poetry) Clifton Snider ($1.00)
-SOMEONE ELSE'S DREAMS(novella) John Yamrus ($4.95)

The above books may be ordered directly from Applezaba
Press, P.O. Box 4134, Long Beach, CA 90804. Please
include 75¢ on each order for postage and handling.
California residents add appropriate sales tax.